To Superhero Sebastian and
beautiful Lara Ruben.
— S.G.

For Susanne, superhero to many.
— M.C-F.

First published 2019

EK Books
an imprint of Exisle Publishing Pty Ltd
PO Box 864, Chatswood, NSW 2057, Australia
226 High Street, Dunedin, 9016, New Zealand
www.ekbooks.org

A CiP record for this book is available from the National Library of Australia.

ISBN 978-1-925335-99-6

Designed by Big Cat Design
Typeset in Clarendon Roman 15/21pt
Printed in China

This book uses paper sourced under ISO 14001 guidelines from well-managed forests
and other controlled sources.

10 9 8 7 6 5 4 3 2 1

3 9957 00211 2841

I

don't

want

glasses.

My parents say that
I look very handsome in them.

I don't want to look
very handsome in them.
They make the backs
of my ears hurt.

Grandma is surprised when she sees me.
'Who's the handsome boy in the big blue glasses?'

'It's me, Sammy.'

'It can't be. You're so handsome.'

Grandpa is very
surprised too.
He asks who the
superhero with
the glasses is.

'It's me, Sammy.'

Grandpa smiles.

'Well, there's a new
superhero in town.'

Aunty Tory comes over and she
doesn't know who I am at all.
'Where's Sammy? I can only see
this handsome boy.'

When I tell her it's me,
she's very excited.

I push them under my bed.

But Ma finds them.

I hide them in my lunch locker.

But Miss May finds them.